Harry
AND THE
JAGGEDY DAGGERS

Jan Fearnley

For all the
Boys and Girls
who work and play
on the North Sea

J.F.

First published in Great Britain 2012
by Egmont UK Limited
239 Kensington High Street
London W8 6SA

www.egmont.co.uk

Text and illustrations copyright
© Jan Fearnley 2012

Jan Fearnley
has asserted her
moral rights

ISBN 978 1 4052 6168 5 (Hardback)
ISBN 978 1 4052 6169 2 (Paperback)

10 9 8 7 6 5 4 3 2 1

46270/1/2

A CIP catalogue record
for this title is
available from
the British Library

Printed and bound
in Malaysia

EGMONT
we bring stories to life

Not very far away,
there's a place where the Winding River
flows into the Big Wide Sea.
There are boats on the water, ships in the harbour
and interesting animals all around.
It's a busy place, a special place – and
its name is Bottlenose Bay.

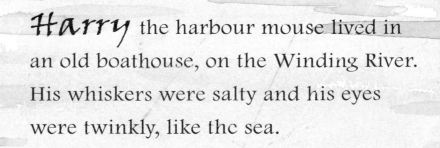

Harry the harbour mouse lived in
an old boathouse, on the Winding River.
His whiskers were salty and his eyes
were twinkly, like the sea.

Every day, Harry transported cargo in his boat.

He liked river life – people coming and going,
big ships, ferries, sailing boats and tugboats.
He loved the magical way the sea and the wind
brought people and things from faraway places.

But the wind and sea
can make mischief too.

THIS
WAY
UP

One night,
when Harry
was asleep, something
terrible happened.

Zephyr, The Wild Wind, rose up
and loosened the rope that
fastened Harry's boat.

The boat drifted away

into the harbour

out to sea

right on to . . .

...the JAGGEDY DAGGERS!

Now, the Jaggedy Daggers were dangerous, mean old rocks.

They lurked just below the surface of the sea, waiting.

Many ships had been wrecked on their cruel spikes.
Harry's boat was smashed to smithereens!
Like ginormous dinosaur teeth, they
crunched that poor boat up.

In the morning

there was nothing left, except
for a few pieces of broken wood.

Harry was heartbroken.

But as well as mischief, the wind and the sea
can bring surprises and treasures too.

One day, as he wandered along the seashore, Harry found a strange thing washed up by the tide.

It was an old, chipped china teacup, with stars painted around the rim.

Harry had an idea.

"This will make a wonderful boat!" he said.

"What a silly thing!"
scoffed the river rats.

Harry didn't care
and in no time at all,
he was back working
on the river
in his new boat.

He delivered a cargo of shells
to Olivia Otter for her magic spells.

"A teacup. How unusual!"
said Olivia.

He ferried Mama Bun to visit her grandchildren.

He took the Pond Children to school.

They wriggled about so much,
the cup nearly capsized!
"It's too squishy!" they said.

It was true, the teacup boat
was very small . . .

. . . and Harry had to avoid
the BIG ships. *Phew!*

One night,

another terrible storm came.

Huge waves crashed against the pier.
The wind howled and whistled.

And a **HUGE** gust of wind
blew Samina Songbird's nest
right out of her tree!

Out fell the eggs
into the stormy water.

"Help!"
cheeped Samina.
"My eggs!"

The waves swept the eggs
way out to sea!

The current was so strong
that it carried them
straight towards . . .

... the JAGGEDY
DAGGERS!

"Help!"

The riverboats were too big
to go near the Jaggedy Daggers.

They would be smashed and bashed to pieces!

Only Harry, in his tiny boat, could save the eggs now.

Harry
rowed
as fast as
he could.

The sea
was rough.

Huge waves
tossed him

this way . . . .

It was hard work, but Harry was determined.

. . . . . and that way.

At last he reached the eggs.

Then, carefully, he used the spoon
to scoop each one out of the water.

His boat tipped and spun!

Harry came dangerously close
to the deadly daggers.

But he kept going until every egg was saved.

At the jetty,
a fantastic flotilla of friends
welcomed Harry home.

"What a hero!"

they cheered.

"Hip, Hip, Hurrah for Harry!"

Harry was presented
with a special reward –
a shiny, big red
tugboat!

So, every day, Harry carried
cargo and passengers
all around the river.
He liked his red tugboat
very much.

Le Grand Fromage

But on special days,

like the day Samina's eggs hatched,
Harry would leave his big boat at home . . .

. . . and sail out in his little teacup.

Because, even though it was small and chipped
and he paddled it with a rusty old spoon . . .

. . . the little teacup boat was Harry's favourite boat of all.